Combination of Words

Flairs and Glairs
Publication House

"Combination of Words"

ISBN No: " 978-93-90799-87-9"
1ˢᵗ Edition
Language – English and Hindi

Flairs and Glairs
Publication House
Regd. Under MSME Act.

Disclaimer

This is a work of fiction and solely represent the thoughts of the corresponding authors of the articles. Our editors have tried their best to edit the content of all the authors and check the plagiarism.
All the write-ups in this book are unique and are only published in this book.
In case any plagiarism or error is found, only the author is responsible alone, and not the publisher or the Compilers.

Cover Designing and Book Formatting
Shubham Shah and Ishani Agarwal

Co Author

Shubham Shah (Founder Flairs and Glairs)
Ishani Agarwal (Co Founder Flairs and Glairs)

1. Riya Rashmi Dash
2. Smita Mohanty
3. Jaspreet Kaur
4. Vikas Soni
5. Prashanna Chettri
6. Neha Kumari
7. Suchismita Ghoshal
8. Vinita Anand
9. Avinash Chandra Jha
10. Tanmayee Pani
11. Preeti Kukreja
12. Amitesh Kumar
13. Aayush Sharma
14. Divya Rajiv Jain
15. Shruti Mahajan
16. Chetan Bansor
17. Piya Kawrani
18. Layashree A.V
19. Rekha Ghanshyam Gaur
20. Mubeena Ameer.A
21. Abhishek Yadav
22. Ravinder Kaur Sokhi
23. Astha Patel
24. Nisha
25. Radhika Chejarla
26. Niraj Yadav
27. Akanksha Sureshrao Nawale
28. Shijin Ravi C

29. Divya Rajiv Jain
30. Samparnna Dalbehera
31. Heisuk
32. Kaushik Das
33. Dalan I Mahrhen Rymbai
34. Sindhu Vishnu
35. Hemant Singh Tanwar
36. Anil Mansuriya
37. S. T. Renuka
38. Jeevitha.S
39. Sangram Santosh Salgar
40. Hadassalyne Khonglah
41. Sanjay Naik
42. Bongi.Akhila
43. Pratham Mittal
44. Ramya M Benakanahalli
45. Abhilash Rout
46. Shruthi Abhinaya
47. Abhishek Nahire
48. Payal Indani
49. Shirin
50. Hasrat
51. Purnima Srivastava
52. Shubhangi Shaily
53. नीलम रानी गुप्ता
54. आदित्य
55. Rupsa Das

Shubham Shah

(Founder- Flairs and Glairs)

Shubham Shah, an entrepreneur at "Flairs & Glairs" a brand with dynamics in events organizing and cultural educational pan INDIA, is a 26yrs old guy who recently has entered the digital platform of imprinting emotions. He has initiated with his own open mic platform to help budding poets and aspiring writers under his brand named as "Teekhe Zasbaaat"

He is a commerce graduate from the Bhagalpur City of Bihar. He states Writing has impersonated him since childhood and he has now been writing for over a decade!

Cooking, on the other hand, is his passion! He also mentions, trying out new things just tickles him!

When asked sir, Why SPICY EMOTIONS?

He smiled and added, "agar jasbaat teekhe na ho toh wo jasbaat kahan" Spices are all that blends! So do his words!

As a chef, he presents to you his dish! Hot and freshly served! Taste it! Feel it! Enjoy it! You can also find his writing in the Book "Teekhe Zasbaaat" and 50+ Co-authored anthologies. With his passion to explore opportunities across Platforms, he is working with keen devotion and We wish him all the very best for his future ventures.

He is Featured in the International Magazine DeMode for his upcoming solo novel.

He is Approved by Ne8x for its Lit Fest, and is a Golden Star Awards 2020 Winner.

He is a India Book of Records Holder for his Anthology Satrang, and has the Grandmaster title by Asia Book of Records, for the same.

He has also been featured in Prabhat Khabar, Dainik Jagran, and a lot of other Newspapers in Bihar for his achievements.

He has been a proud co-author to

India Book Of Records (Title- Black)

World Book Of Records (Title -15 Wonders of Poetries)

India Book Of Records (Title - Aaina)

Vajra World Records Holder (Title - Gustakhi Maaf Hai)

High Range of Records Holder (Title - Gustakhi Maaf Hai)

Indian Book of Records

(Title - Road from Worst to Best)

Share your reviews on his

INSTAGRAM

@spicy_emotions
@shubham4shah

Or via email on

shubham2shah@gmail.com

To stay tuned to his work and opportunities follow his business Handles

INSTAGRAM   FACEBOOK   YOUTUBE

@flairsandglairs
@teekhezasbaaat

WEBSITE:

https://flairsandglairs.in/
https://flairsandglairs.com/

Ishani Agarwal

(Co-Founder- Flairs and Glairs)

Ishani Agarwal hails from the City of Joy, Kolkata.

She is the co-founder of her Community "Teekhe Zasbaaat" and Flairs and Glairs Publication.

Been a Compiler for 45+ Anthologies, she is in the process for more. Co-authored in 150+ Anthologies. She is a India Book of Records Holder, a Vajra World Records Holder, a High Range of Records Holder, an OMG Book of Records Holder, a Bravo Record holder, a Forever Star Book of World Records and an Indian Book of Records Holder.

Approved by Ne8x for its Lit Fest 2020, and Literary Icon 2020. Also a Golden Star Awards Winner 2020.

She has also been awarded with India Star Republic Award 2021, a part of She Awards by Awards Arc and Winner of Nari Samman 2021 by Literoma.

She is also selected as Best Achiever of the Year by AwardsArc and Most Challenging Compiler Award by Spectrum Awards.
She got her first solo Published,a solo Compilation consisting of first 750 contents of hers, titled "Hand That Burnt While Healing".

She has been featured by the National Magazine "Taree Zameen Par" with the title 'unstoppable'.
Also featured in the International Magazine DeMode for her upcoming solo novel, she is proud to write on social issues, and is happy with the love she is receiving.
Connect with her on Instagram: @Ishani_agarwal_quotes / @compilations_so_far

Riya Rashmi Dash

Path of Love

Let's decide a path together
A path where we both are the only travelers
Where we will only have love, care and endless moments
Where we will love each other odds and flaws
Where we will pick each other up in moments of solitudes
And cheer up in moments of ecstatic happiness

A path where we will cross all hurdles together
Where we will have our past with some odds, present with
some moments and future awaiting with bundle of happiness
Where you will be the perfect one for me till the last

Let's make a never-ending beautiful path of love
Where we just crave for each other's love and presence
And live happily with cute beautiful moments ever after.

Smita Mohanty

सफ़र हमरा

हाथों में थाम के तेरा हाथ,
आँखों में सजाके दोनों के मिलने की ख्वाब,
रहना था हुम् दोनों को उम्र भर साथ साथ,
ये मांग रही थी दुआ मेरे रब से में,
 हर दिन ओर हर एक रात।
हुम् दोनों का सफ़र पूरी हो एक दूसरे का बन के सहारा,
ये एक ही छोटी सी आशा हैं हमारे।

इश्क के रंग

उन ख्वाबों से यारी थोड़ी सी गहरी हुई है,
आजकल नींद भी कुछ प्यारी सी हुई है,
ख्याल भी किसी के अक्सर परेशान करते हैं,
ऐसा लगता है इश्क़ की शुरुआत हुई है।

ये दुनिया पहले से थोड़ी बदल सी गई है,
देखने वाली ये नजर अलग हो सी गई है,
मुश्किलों भरा सफर भी आसान सा लगता है,
ऐसा लगता है इश्क़ की शुरुआत हुई है।

जिनसे नफ़रत थी कभी उनसे मोहब्बत हुई है,
अनजान था खुद से ही आज मुलाकात हुई है,
बहुत से सवालों के जवाब हैं मिल गए,
ऐसा लगता है इश्क़ की शुरुआत हुई है।

उनके दीदार की बेताबी में दिल बेकाबू हुआ है,
मनमर्ज़ी करने की जैसे आज़ादी मिल गई है,
इस रंग ने धीरे - धीरे अपने रंग में रंग लिया,
ऐसा लगता है इश्क़ की शुरुआत हुई है।

किसी की बेरुखी भी दिल को छूकर गई है,
उनकी इसी अदा से तो मोहब्बत हुई है,
खुद से ज्यादा किसी पर ऐतबार होने लगा है,
ऐसा लगता है इश्क़ की शुरुआत हुई है।

Vikas Soni

Ishq

The word is enough to describe everything
As bicycle or bike can't run without any of one wheel
Same thing in the love
Relationship depends upon both the character of this
beautiful journey
Ever feel your partner in wind or in patter
Yes, because true love exists.
Love never falls you down
It always seems to be the strongest bond
They ignore the pebbles of their bond
But as we all know Karma
It makes them eventually divided.

Prashanna Chettri

Love, A Journey

Love is a journey where two travelers get into it with so much of
passion and ecstasy to reach a destination called forever
And in a hope to love and to be loved
As no one is born loved, with time we learn to embrace another soul
And thus learn the word called love and feel it deep within
That's how it all starts
You feel all those adrenaline rush and butterflies in your belly
Every song reminds you of them and you blush out of nowhere
Even if you pass someone which would give a whiff of the same
aroma that they use it clicks your mind within a sec and make yu
feel as if they're around
But when one out of the two tends to move out of the rollercoaster
ride and aim for another journey with another traveller for another
destination
That just tears oneself apart
How suddenly those butterflies turn into wasp how suddenly those
adrenaline rush turns into shock and how the whiff of their aroma
weakens you down
How those songs bring tears to your eyes and wet your pillow every
night
Watching the one you love with every ounce of your being loving
someone else hurts the most
But don't ever beg for their presence as where no love resides that
home would no longer be home but rather a house with broken
pieces
It weakens you to your bones to suddenly wake up feeling all empty,
with cracks and bits around you
When people's love comes with condition apply scenes
There you get shattered
But dear yu,if someone wants to leave just set them free
All you can do is either love them forever or make them just a mere
memory

Neha Kumari

A Book with Rose

Even today I used to read that volume,
In her remembrance.
When she left,
She just established my Red blossom on that sheet.

The sheet we last read together.

Even today that soulless rose is relaxing there.
And don't know how many breathes,
I read that volume.

Just in this care, that one day
We will touch again and,
Will resume our tale from the same sheet.

Suchismita Ghoshal

Dusty Road

I cross that dusty road every day,
Just to take a glimpse of you,
That road where our footprints kept,
The memories of our cupped palms carefully.
Maybe our memories are mixed into dust,
But for me it increases my heartbeats till now,
I take long sighs till now closing my eyes,
And grin awkwardly to remember your dimples.
Why don't you look up from your balcony now?
And feel restless like the way you did then?
Why don't yours eyes turn pale after
A series of long gaps or series of long silence?
Questions are brewing the smoke in vain,
Where herbanation keeps the answers secret.
That dusty road of fake promises,
Beguiled the sunrises, beautified the sunsets.
I blame those bewitching wind which,
Dragged me towards this road & to you,
As I was just a puppet of its funshow.
No longer I procrastinate on my pen,
To write of our bond and ponder over our gaze.
Fixating my dreams to scribble every bit of it,
I regularly visit this road with my solitude.
Clueless I am, howl sometimes even in gains,
Sometimes I laugh, even in acute pain.
There is so much untold tales in air,
Which turns into dust by a medium, unfair.
I cross that dusty road everyday once or twice;
Full of love, laughs, smiles, partition and sobs,
To engrave our stories forever, free of any vice.

Vinita Anand

टूटता ख़्वाब

आज एक ख़्वाब ने मुझसे पूछा पूरा करोगे या टूट जाऊं।

अपनी खूबसूरत सी जिंदगी में लाना है या उन नाकाम सपनों की तरह मैं भी छूट जाऊं।

मेरी जिंदगी है आपके हाथों में आपके उन मजबूत इरादों में जो मुझे करेंगे साकार।

लाकर अपने उन सच होते सपनों में जो देंगे मुझे जिंदगी बार-बार।

तभी उसके दिल से आवाज आई.. हां तुझे करूंगा मैं साकार अपने उन मजबूत इरादों से दूंगा जिंदगी तुझे बार-बार.. नहीं तुझे मैं खोना चाहता उन सुंदर सपनों की तरह तुझे भी अपनी जिंदगी में बोना चाहता।

मेरे ख़्वाब तुझे करूंगा मैं साकार अब नहीं टूटने दूंगा तुझे बार-बार..।

तेरे पूरा होने से जुड़ी है मेरी कामयाबी।

मेरे ख़्वाब तुझे अपने अंदर पनपने से ही मिलेगी मुझे खूबसूरत जिंदगानी।

मेरे सुंदर ख़्वाब मैं तुझे पूरा कर सकूं तुझे मैं अपने अंदर जुनून की तरह भर सकूं।

काश करूं मैं अपने टूटे सपने को साकार, दू जिंदगी खुद को मैं एक बार।

मेरे सपने तेरे बेचैन मन में भी होंगे ख़्वाब कई, तेरे पूरे होने के इरादे भी चमक रहे होंगे कहीं ना कहीं।

 तेरे मन की निराशा को मैं जान गया, तेरे पूरे होने की आशा को मैं भाग गया।

तू मेरा शुभचिंतक जो चाहता है मेरा भला, करके अपने टूटे ख़्वाबों को पूरा बनाना चाहता है जीवन मेरा।

 हे मेरे प्यारे मेरे दुलारे मेरे ही अंदर जन्मे मेरे सपने सारे, मेरे ख़्वाब तुझे करूंगा मैं साकार अब नहीं टूटने दूंगा तेरा और अपना सपना बार बार.....।

Avinash Chandra Jha

इश्क़-ए-सफ़र की हसरतें

जब मेरा दिल चाहे तुमसे अलग होना,
कर दूँ उसको अगल खुद से मैं, फ़ौरन हीं
अगर मेरा मन किसी और को सोचे,
मैं अपनी ज़हनी सोच वहीं रोक लूँ ।
गर मेरी नज़रें उठे किसी और के दीदार में,
उसमे भी तेरे हीं अक्स का दीदार हो
मेरे ख्वाबों–ख़यालों की मल्लिका,
तेरे सिवा कोई और बनना चाहे कभी,
ऐसी गुस्ताख़ी कभी मुकम्मल ना हो ।

जब मैं खुद में सांसें भरूँ,
मिले मुझे उसमे भी ख़ुशबू तेरी हीं
तेरे होठों से निकला प्रेम का हर लफ़्ज़,
मेरे लिए हों और मुझपर हीं बरसे।
मेरे दिल की हर धड़कन सिर्फ़
तेरे नाम की हीं नुमाइशें करें
तेरे लिए हीं मेरी बाहें पसरे, और
तुमको आगोश में लेकर हीं इनको समेटूँ ।

कुछ ऐसे हों तेरे करम मुझपे,
के जब भी मैं जागूँ–सूऊँ
तेरी गोद मेरा सिरहाना बने
और तुम अपनी हाथों, निगाहों से
मुझपर प्रेम की पुष्प–वर्षा करो ।

जो गुज़रे वो लम्हे सारे, रफ़्तार में
उन सभी मंज़रों को क़ैद कर लूँ
या तेरी चाहत में सबकुछ रोक दूँ
मैं अपनी तमाम उम्र निहारता रहूँ तुम्हे,
कुछ इस अदा से कि, उनसे
नयन–सुख की परम अनुभूति हो, और
हृदय की गहराइयों में अपनी घर कर लें ।

हो मेरी आख़िरी हसरत पूरी इस तरह, के
जब निकले मेरी आख़िरी साँसें, और
जो मुझे मौत आए तो डालना,
मुझपर आँचल अपना, मेरा कफ़न बनाकर,
जिसे ओढ़कर मेरी आख़िरी नींद सुकून भरी हो ।
कुछ ऐसी हो तुमसे जुदाई मेरी की,
मेरी मौत भी तेरी मोहब्बत की हदें देखकर
दुबारा जीने की हसरतें जन्म ले ॥

Tanmayee Pani

(1)

आओ चलें एक सफर में
इश्क़- ए- दास्तान को करते हुए सलाम;
कहते हैं उसे हम सपनों का राजकुमार,
और हम उसकी हसीन शहजादी;
खुशियों से भरा हुआ एक प्यारा सा आशियाना,
जहां उसके और मेरे बीच न था कोई राज़।

आओ चलें एक सफ़र में,
इश्क़ - ए- दास्तान को करते हुए सलाम,
जहां प्रीत की डोर से बंधे दो पंछी,
नैनों के इशारों से करते शरारत,
और प्यार के लम्हों को संजो रहे,
इसे सुन्दर सा इबादत बना कर,
इश्क़ के अल्फ़ाज़ - ए - सफ़र का देकर नाम।

Preeti Kukreja

(1)

The day he proposed me,
Stars were twinkling with joy,
Angels and fairies all around,
Showering blessings of all gods and goddesses.

He wrapped a blindfold on my eyes,
Took me to the upstairs with care,
To my surprise, when I opened my eyes,
Terrace was beautifully designed.

My happiness knew no bounds,
I walked to see the whole terrace,
Heart shaped balloons and scented candles,
All it made a perfect place and won my heart.

For he knew, I love moon and sky the most,
So he chose the best place to propose,
Suddenly, rose petals were showered on me,
And I started twirling in happiness.

He asked, "How is the surprise? "
I replied, "The best, but for whom? "
He bent down on his knees, with a ring in his hand.

He said, "I want to spend my whole life with you.
Will you be mine forever?"
I was awestruck and numb for a second,
Went to him, accepted the proposal and hugged him.

That was the best day for both of us,

For two souls, finally became perfect soulmates,
Surprised and shocked after a while,
I got to know that it's merely a Dream.

Amitesh Kumar

(1)

न ही नज़्म तुम,
न ही गज़ल हो मेरी...!!
न ही नग्म तुम,
न ही शायरी हो मेरी!!
न ही शमा तुम,
न ही परवाना हो मेरी!!
न ही आशिक़ी तुम,
न ही प्यार हो मेरी...!!

पर दुनिया का फ़साना देखिए

हर शब्द में तुम,
हर कविता में मेरी.!!

एहसास गहरा छोड़ जाते हैं वो अल्फाज़,
जो लबों पे मचलते नहीं!!

हसरते आज भी ,"ख़त" लिखा करती हैं,
बस,"वो" अब उस पते पे न रही!!

Aayush Sharma

मुझे बस तु और तेरा यकीं चाहिए

मुझे बस यही अपना नसीब चाहिए,
मुझे बस तु और तेरा यकीं चाहिए।
आज तु ही एक लफ्ज़ दे दे,
और बस जरा फ़िर वो लम्हा दे दे।
हाथों में बस तेरा हाथ हो,
रुक जाए वो पल जब हम साथ हों,
ना दुनिया बदलनी हैं हमें,
ना तुझे, ना खुद को बदलना हैं,
ना गुजरा वक़्त वापस लाना है,
ना कहीं लौट कर जाना हैं,
अब तो यूं ही उम्र भर साथ-साथ रहना है।
मुझे जिंदगी का हर पल जीना हैं,
यूं ही रोज, हर रोज.
तेरा चेहरा दूर ही सही मगर दिल के करीब चाहिए,

एक कदम तु चल लेना, दो कदम हम चले आएंगे
गुजर जाए ये पल, ये दिन, महीने, ये साल,
सारी उम्र मुझे बस यही नसीब चाहिए
मुझे बस तु और तेरा यकीन चाहिए।

Divya Rajiv Jain

दिल का दिमाग़ से कोई रिश्ता नहीं...

सीखना है तो दिल से सिखों,
दिमाग़ से नहीं,
लिखना है तो दिल से लिखों,
दिमाग़ से नहीं,
चाहना है किसी को तो दिल से चाहो,
दिमाग़ से नहीं,
होना है किसी का तो दिल से हो,
दिमाग़ से नहीं ।

Shruti Mahajan

एक सफर इश्क़ के नाम

एक दिन अकेले थे मैं और तुम।
ज़िन्दगी के सफर ने कुछ वक़्त निकाल कर
 हम दोनों को मिलाया।
यकीं नहीं होता की हमने तुम्हे
अपने आप मैं पाया।
मिलता है इतना सबकुछ हमारा।
जैसे कि दिल ने धड़कन को मिलाया।
वैसे ही अच्छा लगता है तेरा नाम मेरे नाम के साथ जैसे कोई सुबह
जुडी हो किसी हसीन शाम के साथ।
इश्क़ करते है तुजसे तेरे नाम का।
अल्फ़ाज़ जुड़े हो तेरे
और
सफर मेरे नाम का तूझे बनाया।

Chetan Bansor

" वजह क्या थी "

ना थी तन्हाईयां ना कोई मजबूरी थी
आँखों ने आँखों से खेली आंखमिचोली थी
बातों ही बातों में बातें हुई क्या थी
सुनोगे? कि आखिर वजह क्या थी

रूठने मनाने का सिलसिला कुछ लंबा चला
उनके दिल में क्या है हमें कैसे ना पता चला
वादों में झलकती फ़रेबी क्या थी
सुनोगे ? कि आखिर वजह क्या थी

समझने की कोशिश में उलझते चले गए
ना जाने कब कैसे रास्ते बदलते चले गए
फिर अब मंज़िलों की परवाह करनी क्या थी
सुनोगे? कि आखिर वजह क्या थी

किसी और को पाकर अब वो खुश लग रहे थे
सपने सुनहरे किसी और के बुन रहे थे
कुछ नहीं था तो दिखावे की जरुरत क्या थी
सुन लिया? कि आखिर वजह क्या थी

Piya Kawrani

(1)

एक नशे सा लगता है तुम्हारा यू आना और जाना।।
पर अब इस नशे से हमे इतना प्यार हो गया है ...
की होंश में आने को जी नही करता...
और होंश में आके भी क्या करे ।।
क्योकि होंश मैं ना तू हो ।।
ना तुम्हारा एहसास ।।
ना तुमहारी बातें ।।
ना तुमहरा प्यार।

Layashree A.V

Music Love

Sitting by the window,
with a cup of hot tea,
and earphones plugged in,
listening to the favorite songs,
relieves my soul.
These things make me feel alive.
Music, the official
companion of mine in
every problem and solution.
I connect to music like
people get connected to tea.
Being a music addict gives you
the best feeling and a
best friend you could ever deserve.

Rekha Ghanshyam Gaur

<u>"जिंदगी"</u>

पैरों में अगर छाले हैं,
तो मरहम खुद ही लगाना होगा।

दिल में अगर दर्द है,
तो इसे दर्द सहना सिखाना होगा।

जीवन में अगर तकलीफ़ है,
तो भी आगे बढ़ना खुद ही को होगा।।

पंख अगर लहू-लुहान हैं,
तो भी हौंसला खुद ही को रखना होगा।

तन्हाईयों से अगर रास्ते वीरान हैं,
तो भी खुद ही खुद का साथ निभाना होगा।।

गलतियों की माफ़ी अगर दुनिया से ना मिले,
तो भी हमें तो खुद को अपनाना होगा।।

जीने के लिये सौ लोग जोड़ भी लें तो क्या,
आये अकेले हैं, तो अकेले ही जाना होगा।

Mubeena Ameer.A

Love is Like Rain

Harrypotter !!
The Name My Rain Called off ...
Its Knows Well ...
My happy and Cheerful Times.
From the Time I Feel in Love till The Time I Cried After Break Up
Every time Rains.
I start Narrate My story
It's Been Six Years
"On a Starry Night
In Some Random Street
When Our Eyes Meet
You steal my smile
When our souls feel in love
Place between Heaven nd Earth
Before It starts. You left.! "
But you are the one who even recognize My Tears in Rain,
 Where Many fails.
After you left
I forget the world
Suddenly I realized there was a heavy storm,
"The storm was shaking the destiny
Under the vast sky,
started to heavy rain
As the Rain drops gently touched me
I Just recollect our memories
My heart beats fast
My tears run down the cheeks
Where Everyone is busy with searching shelter
I stuck with our flashback and memories.
Forever Together is an Illusion...!!!
This rain remains all of this ....

Abhishek Yadav

Knockout

खूबसूरत इतनी है वो ,
कि परियों सी दिखती है ।
चांद भी लेता है बलाएं ,
जब गलियों से निकलती है ।
हवाएं थम सी जाती हैं ,
आग भी देख के जलती है ।
जैसे सुबह का सूरज आया हो ,
चांद को पहरा देने ।
इस तरह उसके चेहरे पर वो बिंदी लगती है ।
जाम फ़ीका सा लगता है ,
उसकी नज़रों के आगे ।
शराब की बोतल भी नशे में हिलती है ।
खूबसूरत इतनी है वो ,
कि परियों सी दिखती है ।।
जिस्म जैसे कि मोम और आग का मिश्रण ,
पर देखकर दिल को बड़ी ठंडक सी मिलती है ।
ये आदत हो गई है मदिरा पान सी ,
उसे देखकर ही अब मेरी हर शाम ढलती है ।
ऐसा वार किया उसने ,
नज़रों की धार से ।
उसे देखता हूं बस तभी आराम मिलती है ।
खूसूरत इतनी है वो ,
कि परियों सी दिखती है ।।
वो भी समझे मेरे जज़्बात तो कुछ बात बढ़ चले ,
मैं कुछ कह नहीं पाता उससे ये मेरी ही गलती है।

हंसती है वो ऐसे कि कलियों सी खिलती है ।
बड़ी शैतान हैं उसकी काली मेघ सी जुल्फ़ें ,
बार - बार चेहरे पर आकर गुलाबी अधरों से मिलती हैं ।
खूबसूत इतनी है वो ,
कि परियों सी दिखती है ।।

मैरी तरह

हां, ये सच है कि मैं एक मुद्दत से अकेला हूं ,
इस दुनिया के मेले में एक छोटा सा ठेला हूं ।।
तुझे जो मानना है मान , मैं पागल, मैं आंवारा ,
मगर नज़रें उठा के देख मैं चारों ओर फैला हूं ।।

तू कहती है , नहीं कर सकता मैं परवरिश तेरी ।
ज़रा नज़रें झुका के देख ,
मैं उस दीमक का टीला हूं ।
जो अंदर है समेटे चांद , सूरज और तारों को ।
मैं वो आकाश हूं जो चाह में तेरी अकेला हूं ।
ज़रा नज़रें उठा के देख ,
मैं चारों ओर फैला हूं ।

Ravinder Kaur Sokhi

The Journey

Sky is showering himself,
The winds stealing the smell of dust,
touches everyone gently.
The Thunder and Lightning are
dancing together....
Rewinding the time....

From embracing myself to weep in the rains
To Dance in the rain remembering you,
I befriended myself.

From bidding Wish
To finding Wish in monsoon,
I fell in love with myself.

From hiding all my feelings like the red skies
To pour out like an opaque rain,
I dared to look straight in my heart.

From standing like a lifeless statue
To smiling with my eyes and mind wet
saying your name,
I fall for you again and again....

Looking towards the skies,
Hoping to have you besides me...
You never faded.......

My journey of a decade,

I had your shadows with me.
I wish a day to come,
When I will be bewitched
with those magical eyes of yous.
And Rains will be pouring on us.

Wish! I wish you feel the Monsoon,
I have in my heart throughout,
The Exile of your Love

Astha Patel

Still Rain Evokes Me

In the black night it started raining
Your memories did some Intrigue,
Today I am suddenly missing you
Probably it's going to rain again...
Come back, I miss you!
am burning in your distance some were
May be some fire is still pressurized in my heart,
It's a petition come back
So that it can again get engaged.
That first sigh!
Took my heart away from me,
I haven't forgot your shelter till now
In which I lived for years...
yours clinging to me before getting apart
The helpless eyes still complain me,
That smile comes in front of my eyes
Making me more cherished,
Sometimes I forget you
But these raindrops ruin every tries of mine,
The rain misses you a lot
Today also it talks about you with me,
One umbrella and two hands holding each other
The sip of tea under stall with snowy winds blowing,
It's difficult to make my soul understand
That it was just a dream that went on flowing...

Yes, I Am Hurt

A sense of loneliness deep within, broken and shattered, losing
every bit of thing that ever mattered. falling apart from the path
I followed, losing a heart that was left so hollowed. yes, I am
hurt!
Don't know how secretly the fate played,
I totally got betrayed.
I scream inside but I can't speak. For love.
The strength I have is what makes me weak. For love.
To end in you is what my heart seeks.
Yes, I am hurt. I love in hell and heavy is my heart...
There were some yearnings of grief in talking,
Whatever happened to me neither I know nor my heart,
No one know how hurt I am...
The thread was weak that's why it broke in a moment,
 For Loved ones Self-aggrandizement
My happiness is not mine anymore!
In the way of faithfulness, I am lost
At every turn I was isolated!
Yes, I am hurt,
My heart's courtyard is filled with silence
Deep inside i am lonely,
Searching for your glance,
When someone asks me how I am?
My soul bursts into tears saying " I am hurt"...

Nisha

(1)

शिकायते कम हो गयी हैं मुझसे,
शायद अब उम्मीदे कही और लगने लगी है..

पता तो मुझे भी था लोग बदल जाते है,
मगर मैने तुम्हे उन लोगो में गिना ही नहीं था

काश तोड़ पाते हम अपना दिल
और दिल से उसकी मोहब्बत खत्म हो जाती,
जो यादे कही दबी थी उसकी
वो भी साथ में उसके चली जाती.

कैसे बयान करूँ अपना इश्क़ अल्फाज़ो में,
आती नहीं नींद रातों में,
खो से जाते हैं तेरे ख्यालों में,
कभी उलझे से सवालो में

कभी जो मुझे फ़तवाह देने का मौका मिले,
तो मै किसी को बेपनाह प्यार करने के बाद
छोड़ कर जाना हराम लिख दू.

तू जरुरी है मुझे हर जरुरत से ज्यादा,
तेरी प्यास है मुझे पानी से ज्यादा,
कैसे साथ छोड़ दू तेरा,
तेरी जरुरत है मुझे मेरी साँसों से ज्यादा

वो चाय सा कड़क,
मैं बिस्कुट सी नर्म,
डूबे उसके इश्क़ में तो
आखिर एक दिन टूटना ही था.

टूट जाते थे तारो की तरह हम
उसकी हर दुआ पूरी करने के लिए
इस उम्मीद में कि एक दिन उनकी दुआ पूरी होगी
और हम एक हो जायेंगे

लेकिन हमे क्या पता था होगी दुआ
अगर उनकी पूरी तो वो किसी और के हो जायेंगे.

कुछ इस कदर अपनी वफ़ा निभाएंगे,

वो छोड भी गया तो प्यार में किये
सारे वादे अकेले निभायेंगे.

Uski ek muskan par Hum kurban hain
Uski ek muskan par Hum kurban hain

Par khair jane do
Kyuki wo kisi or ki jaan hain.

Koi kare izhar-e-ishq to
Smbhal kar ikrar karna mere yaar,

Ye sardi ka mausam hain
Aksar log isme behek jaya karte hai.

Radhika Chejarla

Hands of Mine

I clean my cupboard.
Wash hands.
Without, saying by any.
Books are kept in bag.

No one feeds me.
Actually, none bothers about it.
Even I am afraid of dark.
Can only hold my hand.

Several questions in this heart.
Silence says yes.
My tears also have value.
Why don't you understand?

Want to see mother.
Many told we don't know.
It hurts a lot.
All notice smiles.
But not hidden pain.

Our Eyes Are Wrong.

We human being
Are so busy
Forget tiny things
Of happiness.

Bringing smile on
One's face.
Is not that difficult.

A pure smile on
there face.
Says how beautiful
World is.

Interaction makes
you to feel closeness.
Being kind.
Is really needed.
Dust is not them
Our eyes it is.

Humanity.

I'm a shopkeeper and my name are anand. We sell toys for kids. I love watching them while taking toys some spark will be noticed on kids. It was afternoon, a boy and little girl started crying. Suddenly, she crying became so loudly which made my eyes to see her. She is in brown dress with pink cheeks.
Every day, the boy used to come and see my shop. After a week, he got disappeared. I forgot that thing and concentrated on selling. A customer came to my shop for purchasing a cool doll to her beautiful daughter. She happily chooses one. He comes all of a sudden and grabs that doll from her by saying it's my sister's. I don't know how to react. From his pocket took three hundred rupees and kept on table. I asked him, do you know how much does it costs? No, all I know is my sister wants it. If money is more take it that also. He ran and gave it her sister. A pure smile can attract anyone. I called him and gave money which he kept on table. And said take it for free. He told no need I don't want it for free. My mom said not to take things like this. So, from tomorrow I will come and work and pay the remaining. I loved his innocence.

Meanwhile, my customer who was watching all this. Appreciated me and convinced her daughter to take another doll.
He also promises that going to take care of that boy and her sister.
Then I felt humanity still exists.

Niraj Yadav

<u>तू जोर से छलांग लगाले</u>

जो बीतना था सो बीत गया,
अब तो पढ़ाई पर ध्यान लगाले।
कुछ वक्त और बचा है,
तू जोर से छलांग लगाले।
हाथ-पर-हाथ रखें,
निर्भर मत हो अपने तक़दीर पर।
उठ, मेहनत कर, और
मत बैठाकर हमेशा मन्दिर पर।

कड़ी मेहनत और लगन से,
तू अपना किस्मत संवार ले।
कुछ वक्त और बचा है,
तू जोर से छलांग लगाले।
सब तुम पर आस लगाये बैठे हैं,
'तू सफल होगा' इसका विश्वास दिला दे।
कुछ वक्त और बचा है,
तू जोर से छलांग लगाले।

Akanksha Sureshrao Nawale

Positive Outlook.

I know it's toughest time
No chance to survive and to shine.
Still having faith in self
Anyway, don't lose your cool mind.
Transparently I say, It's toughest time.

You need to proceed with hope,
Leaving hypocrisy behind -
and counting folk.
Pulling adversity by sarcastic joke,
However, we perform and react;
have noteworthy scope.

Coz I know; It's toughest time
No chance to survive and to shine.

Shijin Ravi C

My Next Breath

It's that day again,
To this world all alone,
With none known to all my own,
Year after year made me moult,
That a day counted my age,
All that I did just flashed around,
With talks and gifts all around,
None to avoid nor to hate,
Made them present a wonderful day,
On twelve at midnight just like clock,
Waked me up to one step ahead of old,
With all the love and their care,
I still live within their sweet tears.

Divya Rajiv Jain

(1)

Birthday comes around 365 days in a year,
But person like my friends is only comes once in a life as a lifetime,
I am so glad & I am too much lucky to have you a friend like you i.e., the original one,
In this world everything is copied but friendship never copied...
Best wishes on my friend special day.

Samparnna Dalbehera

Celebrate to Thank Our Existence

When I was a kid, I was so obsessed with jollification of birthdays. Like new dresses, cakes, candles, wishes, scads of gifts and lot of my friends. A huge special day celebration. My parents had decided to celebrate my birthday in every five years. I always had a grumble of my birthday not being celebrated every year but, I was jovial. In every five years, a grand arrangement was being done with hundreds of guests and with whole of my family tree. I used to get lot of presents. I was very happy inside out. Being a kid, these things were my dosage of ecstasy.

Then with the evolution of time I started disliking all of these crazy dramas. Rather I preferred celebrations limited to family members. Less like a birthday but more like a family get-together. There wasn't a lot of gifts though but all that mattered was the physical presence of near and dears. I was eternally elated.

As I grew up, I didn't like my birthdays to be celebrated like why to celebrate a day when you are stepping a year ahead to your doom's day.

Then with the moment of time I realized birthdays weren't just special day but its way beyond. Every year of birthday is a symbol of our successful existence in this Universe. Now I celebrate my birthday by lighting same number of diyas as of my age and thank Almighty for this amazing life. These days my birthdays aren't eye grabbing celebrations but a tiny arrangement which really touches my heart.

Birthdays are very momentous which celebrates our successful survival.

Heisuk

(1)

My wish
I was born in march,
Thanking God for Another year of life happy birthday to me.

Kaushik Das

(1)

Your write-up with title *
I can see the celebrations of stars
From my garden
But I can't see the moon

May be the moon is afraid of my eyes
My eyes are occupied by dried tears

Dalan I Mahrhen Rymbai

Wishes

Best Wishes to you
On this happy moment,

Live life doing, what you love.
Not what impresses others.

Whatever with the past has gone,
The best is always yet to come.

May you have a wonderful life,
With happiness all the way.

Let it be fantastic, crazy.
Wonderful, unbelievable and unforgettable.

May peace, health and happiness be with you,
In every walk of your life.

Wishing you a long healthy life

Sindhu Vishnu

Celebration

The action of celebrating an important day in our life. It is a social gathering spot or enjoyable activity held to celebrate something. Remembering the special occasions of special ones is a milestone. Celebrate your life with your own lights. Celebrating success, it doesn't mean that u r failure in fail. Celebration is one of the achievements in success. We must celebrate our success with our special ones. Now a days due to this corona they are not celebrating because we need our lives than celebration. We live we can celebrate many more achievements in future.

Hemant Singh Tanwar

Mother's Day!

every day of my life has your essence maa,
i won't grow apart from you, it's my promise maa.
simplicity is your identity,
you are God's reflectivity.
solitary confinement may petrify me,
but I'm aware that your blessings will protect me.
oftentimes I get upset with you maa,
but trust me, your love rejuvenates me maa.
presences of members in house signifies peace and love,
but presence of you makes it home of peace and love.
let me flourish your life with all the love, let me repay your
efforts with my success,
it's all I've asked god in my prayers.
please forgive me for my sins,
i won't let you down, to you I'll be the best kin.
Wish you a,
HAPPY MOTHER'S DAY MAA!
every day of my life has your essence maa,
i won't grow apart from you, it's my promise maa.

Anil Mansuriya

Happy Birthday My Bestee Chiky

To my dearest most caring bestee. Wish you very very happy birthday Chikuuuuuuudaaaaaaaa(geet bhiyajiya) My kinda weirdo my sizuuuuuuuuu . Words can't describe you chiku at least I can't bcoz you are special to me very special & you are just best no words can define what you are to me. If I were asked to tell something about us then this would be that.

If I am mad, you are the one can handle me. If I have gone crazy then you are the one who adds to that & make the moment crazier. If I am sad then you are the one who can bring that idiotic funny smile again on my face. If I'm happy then you add to my happiness. If I am angry then you are the one who calms me down. In short you are a perfect complete gift of mine and I love you lottt bestee.

Yes, I don't show it out much but I do I do a lot.

Just remember always what yours is mine what's mine is your so our happiness lies within us.

And hahahahaha our friendship is unique, amazing and so beautiful words can't describe us.

Thank you for being there for me always and I know you will be there for me no matter how much we fight.

Thank you for listening to me always without complaining about anything.

Thank you so much for handling all my mood swing my irritated texts all my madness and there is no one in this world. Who can handle me this way but I am happy that I have one. beautifully coming soon completed one years of our friendship. I am proud that me & you best friend.

S. T. Renuka

Birthday Wish:

You are shielded by the sky
Followed by the sun, moon
and the stars...!
You are strong; courageous;
and of course, yes
You are a born leader!!
Happy Birthday:-)

Jeevitha.S

It's My Fairy's Birthday!

It's her day,
It's the day when she was born before years;
It's the day a family brought out a fairy into this world,
This fairy made everyone's life happier through her presence,
This fairy nevertheless showed her love and care and also made people feel special.
In the same way she stepped into my life and made it a best part through her love,
When her presence meant so much,
Her absence would even make us feel unalive,
It's my magical fairy, whom I love so much,
On this day I pray for your wellbeing;
And thank your parents for such a gift that they gave to us.

Sangram Santosh Salgar

Birthday

Everyone comes
Everyone wishes you

Your birthday is full of joy
All are making enjoy

All blessings are with you
But birthday date only knew few

Your birthday special for everyone
Everyone is eagerly waiting for your celebration

Celebration gives happiness
Your birthday gives love to everyone

Wishing you happy birthday
Always be happy...

Hadassalyne Khonglah

Birthday

On your birthday I wish you full of success. Never give up because I see a remarkable greatness in you. May your life be blessed with great happiness. May God be your guiding light and may he always protect you from all the difficulties in life.......

Sanjay Naik

Birthday!!

On this auspicious occasion of birthday, I wish God only that
happiness doubles you
wish you a bright future.

Smile be on your face all the time
May all your wishes be fulfilled
May your flight of dreams be very high
and your majesty be immense.

May your health be better and no disease can touch you
May your wishes be fulfilled
I just wish that.

Bongi.Akhila

Life Is A Delicious Celbrtion

Birthday is beautiful celebration,
Celebrations are indicators Happiness
What is lost and won in life should be accepted as a
celebration,
Festival is the foundation of enthusiasm,
There is no life without celebration.,
The festival is not only an address to happiness but also an
assurance of support in danger,
Festivals give motivation to move forward in life,
Festivities are the weapons that put an end to heart-
wrenching consciousness,
Celebrations are signs that success in life is ahead,
Birthday is the day when the parents who gave us life gave us
a better understanding of birth,
We cry on our birthday, which is the first celebration of our
lives,
The day of the dead, which is the last festival in our lives,
will cry for those who thought of us,
That is the beauty of life journey,
Pure happiness is always measured in every heart that seeks
the happiness of others,
Vapors of joy are the drops of the festival ... Even the
teardrops are the dewdrops of the festival,
The festival is a symbol of unity
A serene heart is the ideal for a true celebration...

Ramya M Benakanahalli

Birth + Day = The Day of Born.

Born from Mom's womb,
It's a day of my birth.
I'm special to my parents,
They are my gifts of life.

The day I born, I cried and
Mom cried.
The day I born, festive
In my home.
The day I born with tears,
My mom with pain.
The day I born she gave
Me the breath and aim
Breathing with her grace.
This was the real celebration,
This birthday is unforgettable.

"Cutting cake, blasting the party pop, presenting gifts etc........, is not the real celebration of born day, thanking mom & dad for a special day, taking their blessings is one of the best gifts of birthday"

Thank you

Abhilash Rout

Birthday

We come across different phases of life,
but the important of all is the stage of
birthday celebration.
We celebrate birthday very happily as we
know that we have added year in my life,
but simultaneously we forget that we come
one year closer to our death.
Birthday adds blessings to our life,
as we celebrate them with our loved ones.
It brings immense pleasure in our lives,
as we become one year elder in strength,
wisdom, strength and blessings.
Birthday always brings blessings to our life,
we should promise ourselves to change all
the negativity within us in the coming
birthday as we really don't know that after
which birthday our eyes will completely be
closed forever.

Shruthi Abhinaya

A Wish for My Sister:

I'm still clueless that she turned 17 now. Cause I still remember those small tiny little fingers of holding mine. When I saw her for the 1st time i felt like a small package size angel doll came into our house for me to play with. You know how happy I was, I remember each n every little thing she did. No matter how bad she behaved, I still cared for her like a mom does. I holded her hand on day 1 and I promise I'll never leave her hand until the very last breath of mine.
I'll have her back and will be looking at her shine brightly from far. I'm sorry for being rude at times. I love you; I'll love you no matter where u is, how u are.
I can't even imagine my life without this precious lil sister god had gifted me 17yrs back. Whatever you do, you are still my charming little princess.

More than being a sister, I felt deep inside myself as a mother to you.

Abhishek Nahire

I wish

She screams all the words
I wish
I could shout out from the roof top

In a melody that both soothes me and reminds me of all I try
to forget

Either way I listen to her speak, the volume too high my ears
feel like they'll pop.

I lose my thoughts to her voice, drown my questions away,
with each tune, with every beat.

Payal Indani

Unpredictable Life

People may come, people may go.
All the way from their heart, there love will flow.
Yawning to sleeping, you will fall for the one.
Accidently you will start approaching the one.
Loving him, will soon become the best part of your life.
Words are always written from heart.
Raising our passion most effective and smart.
Immensely loving someone is all we can do.
Teaching the opponent to love you too.
Enjoying every moment of life.
Rather it be happy or sad, just live it within and survive.

Shirin

(1)

पता नहीं क्यों,
प्यार का रंग मेरे श्रृंगार का हिस्सा बनते जा रहा हैं
जानती हूं मैं, मंजूर नहीं होगा ये दुनिया को
पर मेरा दिल इस प्यार के रंग में रंगते ही जा रहा है
शर्माना ना आया जिसको
देखो आज उसके चहरे पर ये शर्म खिलते ही जा रहा है
ये प्रेम का रंग है
ये एक कली को अपने रंग में रंगते ही जा रहा है।

Hasrat

(1)

One of the saddest aspects of growing up is the distance that grows between fantasy and reality. when sensibility strikes in, our favourite song turns out to be the disliked one, not because of feelings attached but because of the new beats substituting it soo well, that we start questioning ourselves, "this was something I admired??" People tend to put labels to the cycle of change which knocks at their doors for a ride to make their future, a place where they can accept themselves, don't know why they neglect their feelings...?? Adolescence, mental transitions, relationship alterations, people often perceived these opportunities as the unfavorable phase of their life complaining about the pros and cons of their existence in which cons are always attached to their perspective which are established by society.

18-year-old me was wondering how could I offend the transitions which were a part of life, worrying about the scars it will leave behind after battling with my efforts to vanish them.

Spoiler: (basically not the scars but the fear of new beginnings) In the research of "How can I stop worrying ??" I came across a quote popping up as an advertisement to some new series of books," Fear Has A Large Shadow but Himself Is Small" An unexpected stimulus hits the cluster of my nerve cells resulting in communication through synapses. As I dig into the sequel of sayings, sliding one by one, my heart started to ponder over the glimpses of the past, the circumstances when I suppressed an emotion called fear, you know judging the movie before the interval...!!! How many times, I debited its account, hiding behind the curtains, choosing not to perform. Isn't that ironic...?? we always judge every strand of life, finding ways

to blame the luck and the ungrateful destiny while defending the wrong departures, we always choose to be on the safe side of the fence, why?? Because somewhere deep inside we all ignore the advice of guardian of fear that stands beside us in every risky situation, to guide us through the finish line, we just need to walk towards it with the eyes of a warrior, not a victim.

"They quote it fear, I call it my wears because it's the only thing which keeps me magnetizing to the verge of me, being real."

Purnima Srivastava

<u>माशूका</u>

बस यूँ ही ज़िंदगी का सफर कुछ हसीन लोगों के साथ हसीन बन
जाता है,
तेरी अदाओं का कहना,
ये दिल तो हर बार तेरी निगाहों में डूबकर रह जाता है।

मंज़िल के बारे में मै ज्यादा सोचता नहीं,
बस तेरा साथ सुहाना लगता है।

सुभानल्लाह! किस्मत ने माशूका मेरी जो तुझे बनाया है,
मेरे लाख ज़ख़मों पर मरहम लगाने का उसका इरादा लगता है।।

Shubhangi Shaily

(1)

सुना है, आज वही लोग तुम्हारे अजीज़ बने बैठे है
जिनसे कभी तुम किया करते थे नफरत,
आखिर यही तो है तुम्हारी फितरत।

याद है मुझे,तुम्हारा उन्हें नापसंद करना,
बात बात पर उन्हें भला बुरा कहना।

अरे!!!!!
ज़रा सोचो ना कितने बड़े फरेबी हो,
ना तब उनके थे ना अब उनके हो।
याद है मुझे तुम्हरा कहना,कि तुम्हे उनकी जरूरत नहीं,

पर देखो ना,
तुम्हारी जरूरतें भी आज होती हैं उन्हीं से पूरी।
अजीब बात है न!
आज वही लोग तुम्हारे हमदर्द बने बैठे है,
जो कभी हुआ करते थे तुम्हारे लिए सरदर्द।

अब उनलोगो से क्या कहूं कि कितने मुनाफ़िक़ हो,
आज उनके तो कल किसी और के आशिक़ हो।

माना ये फरेबी, ये मुनाफक़त तुम्हारी हकीक़त है,
पर उनका क्या जिन्हें इनसे शिकायत है?

नीलम रानी गुप्ता
आजादी

मत कहो तुम लड़की हो,
जब सड़कों पर चलती हो।
नहीं अधिकार सिर्फ पुरुष का,
ये हक तुम भी रखती हो।।
है अधिकार संजोएं सपने,
रखें हौंसले बुलंद भी अपने।
जन्म एक सी भाँति सबका,
फिर कम कैसे हो सकती हो।।
लिंग भेद है हीन भावना,
कहो नहीं है तुम्हें मानना।
जो कर सकता कुछ पुरुष वही सब,
कहो तुम भी कर सकती हो।।

आदित्य

मैं और तुम

हर दुख पर भारी होगी मुस्कान तुम्हारे होंठों की
हर सुख की हितकारी होगी मुस्कान तुम्हारे होंठों की
रोती आंखों को मिल जाए मौसम हँसने रोने के
तुमसे मिल कर जीने के और बंधन सब खो देने के

इतना अकेला जीवन भी दूर से सुंदर लगता है
रूदन जो अपने मन का है हँसने से बेहतर लगता है
इस सुर्ख सुनहरी दुनिया में एक प्रश्न के जैसे जीवन का
तुम और मैं ही एक उत्तर हैं अक्सर ऐसा लगता है

मिट्टी होती दुनिया अपनी राज महल हो जाएगी
सब कुछ खोती दुनिया अपनी कोहिनूर जब पाएगी
केवल गीतों पर ही दुनिया अपनी कायल है
तुमको मेरे संग जो देखे तो पागल हो जाएगी

Rupsa Das

(1)

Anjaan bheed mein kho maat jana,
Mujhse durr kabhi ho na jana.
Mohabbat si ho gayi hai tumse,
Toh phir alvida keh ke kabhi chale na jana.

(2)

Kuch baatein haseen si reh jati hai,
Kuch baatein ankahi si reh jati hai.
Kuch baatein zubaan pe aake ruk jati hai,
Kuch baatein sirf dil dhadkati hai

Flairs and Glairs, a platform by a student for the students. We are esteemed youth struggling to carve out our path for our future and we follow a basic mindset Since everyone is not born with all-round skills. Joining hands with people who are born to execute it with perfection is the best way to evolve. Self-Evolution is the need of the hour but, evolving as a community is what we strive for. The initiative as kickstarted by, Founder- Mr. Shubham Shah with the motive to utilize the skillset and talent of writing has now a team of 10+ people who are actively participating into newer forms of learning and discovering talents among youngsters. We Provide platform and services like Publishing opportunities, Open mics, Workshops, Hands-on training. Operating with Brand Name of Flairs and Glairs (Publication House), we offer the chance of elevating a passionate writer to an esteemed author With Brand name Teekhe Zasbaaat. We bring to you an opportunity to get accustomed with the Public Speaking and Presenting of Thoughts along with regular challenges to brush up your inking spirit. The newest initiative to extend our services we introduced in a new writing Platform- The Glittering Fables and Ink Over Tears.

We Choose to Fly Like A Falcon than to be

a Leg Pulling Crab.

To Know More: Infoline – 7781900870
Mail Us At-
flairsandglairs@gmail.com / info@flairsandglairs.in
Or Visit is at
www.flairsandglairs.com / www.flairsandglairs.in
Social Handles- @flairsandglairs @teekhezasbaaat